Sheep Blast Off!

Written by **Nancy Shaw**

Illustrated by **Margot Apple**

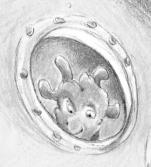

Houghton Mifflin Company
Boston 2008

To Kathy, Jim, Elly, Lotfi, Jim, and Marnie   —N.S.

For Grayson and Ella Rizzi and cousin Francis   —M.A.

Text copyright © 2008 by by Nancy Shaw
Illustrations copyright © 2008 by Margot Apple

The text of this book is set in Garamond.
The illustrations are colored pencil.

www.houghtonmifflinbooks.com

Library of Congress Catalog Number 2007034290
ISBN-13: 978-0-618-13168-6

Printed in Singapore
TWP 10 9 8 7 6 5 4 3 2 1

Sheep see a shape in the mist, by a tree.

Something has landed! What can it be?

Sheep snoop. Sheep explore.

Sheep climb through the spaceship door.

Sheep stumble. Sheep bumble.

Engines slowly start to rumble.

They grab a knob. It seals the door.

Lights come on. Engines roar.

Everyone gets into gear.
They blast right through
the stratosphere.

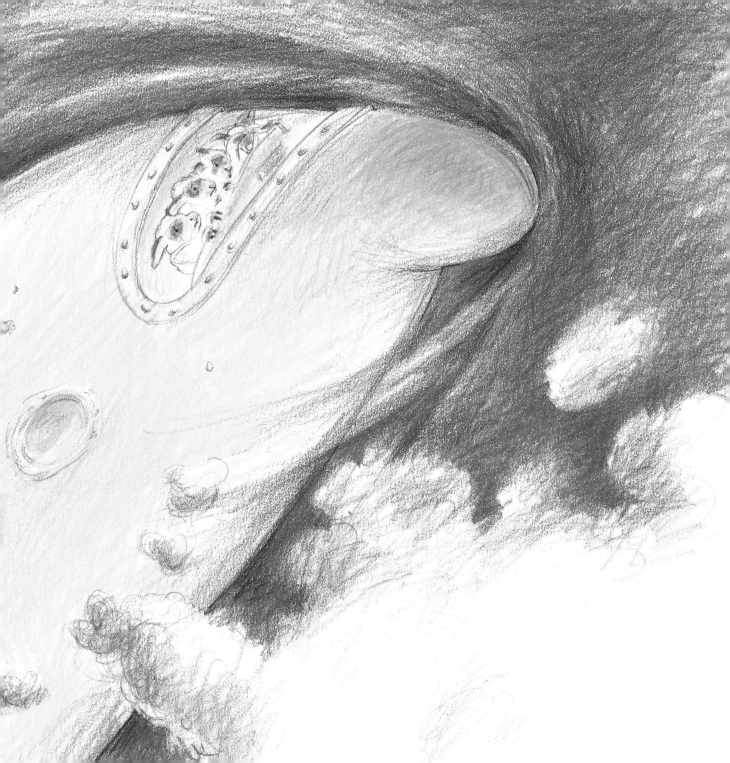

Around the world
the rocket zips.
Weightless sheep
do jumps and flips.

What's that thump? They hit the deck.

Two sheep float

outside to check.

There's just a scratch.

It looks okay.

Back through the hatch—

they're on their way.

They tinker with the main controls.

The rocket lurches, swoops, and rolls.

Lights flash.

Computers beep.

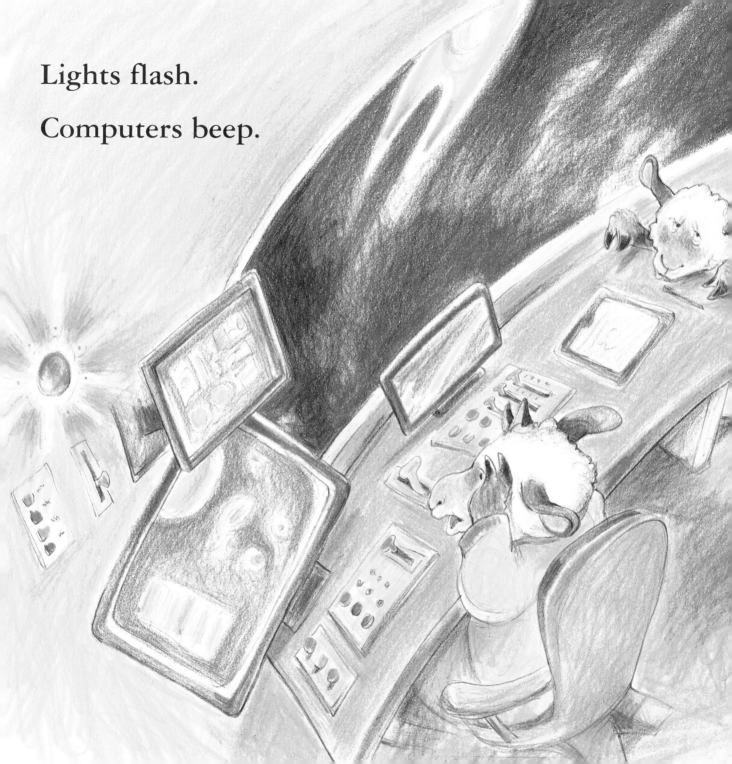

Blaring sirens scare the sheep.

Sheep panic. Sheep guess.

Which button should they press?

Autopilot! That's the one!

Leaving orbit! Nicely done!

Prepare for touchdown!

Home at last!

Rocket sheep have had a blast.